Q: Why did the cat sleep under the car?
A: Because he wanted to wake up oily.

Q: Why did the cat sleep
A: A terrified postman!

Q: Why did the cat cross the road?

A: It was the chicken's day off!

Q: How do you make cats furry?

A: The spin cycle.

Q: When is a lion not a lion?
A: When he turns into his cage!

Q: Why is the cat so grouchy?
A: Because he's in a bad mewd.

Q: For a man to truly understand rejection.
A: He must first be ignored by a cat.

Q: How do you make cats furry?
A: The spin cycle.

Q: What do you call a flying cat?
A: I'm-paws-sible.

Q: What do tigers wear in bed?
A: Stripey pyjamas!.

Q: Why did the cat wear a dress?
A: She was feline fine.

Q: How do cats end a fight?
A: They hiss and make up.

Q: What does a cat like to eat on a hot day?
 A: A mice cream cone.

Q: What did the cat say when he lost his toys?
A: You got to be kitten me.

Q: Why was the cat sitting on the computer?
A: To keep an eye on the mouse!

Q: Who delivers presents to cats?
A: Santa Claws!.

Q: How do you make a cat happy?
A: Send it to the Canary Islands!

Q: What do you call a cat that bowls?
A: An alley cat!

Q: What did the alien say to the cat?
A: Take me to your litter.

Q: What is a cat's favorite color?
A: Purrrple!

Q: What do cats wear at night?
A: Paw-jamas!

Q: What is a cats favorite musical instrument?
A: Purr-cussion.

Q: What do you call a cat that lives in an igloo?
A: An eskimew!

Q: What do you call a cat on ice?
A: One cool cat.

Q: Why are cats better than babies?

A: Because you only have to change a litter box once a day.

Q: What is a feline's favorite day of the week?

A: Caturday.

Q: What do you call a cat that can address the media?
A: A Press Kit.

Q: What do you call a painting of a cat?
A: A paw-trait.

Q: What time is it when ten cats chase a mouse?
A: Ten after One.

Q: What do you call a cat that does tricks?
A: A magic kit.

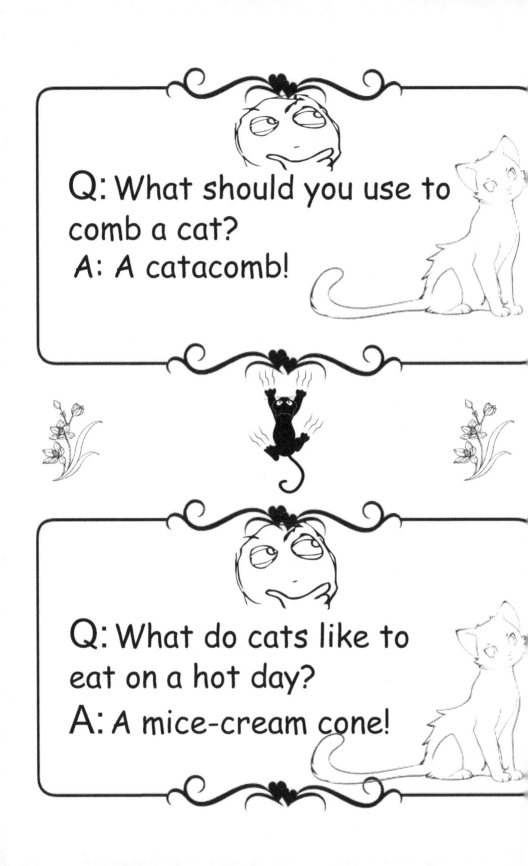

Q: What should you use to comb a cat?
A: A catacomb!

Q: What do cats like to eat on a hot day?
A: A mice-cream cone!

Q: How do two cats end a fight?
A: They hiss and make up!

Q: What's a cat's favorite magazine?
A: Good Mousekeeping!

Q: Why did the cat wear a fancy dress?
A: She was feline fine!

Q: What's a cat's favorite color?
A: Purr-ple!

Q: Why was the cat afraid of the tree?
A: Because of its bark!

Q: What did the cat say when it was confused?
A: I'm purr-plexed!"

Q: Why was the cat so agitated?
A: Because he was in a bad mewd!

Q: What did the cat say when it was confused?
A: I'm purr-plexed!"

Q: How is cat food sold?
Usually
 A: purr the can!

Q: What do baby cats always wear?
A: Diapurrs!

Q: Why are cats great singers?

A: Because they're very mewsical!

Q: Why can't cats play poker in the jungle?

A: Too many cheetahs!

Q: What's another name for a cat's house?
 A: A scratch pad!

Q: What do cats use to make coffee?
A: A purr-colator!

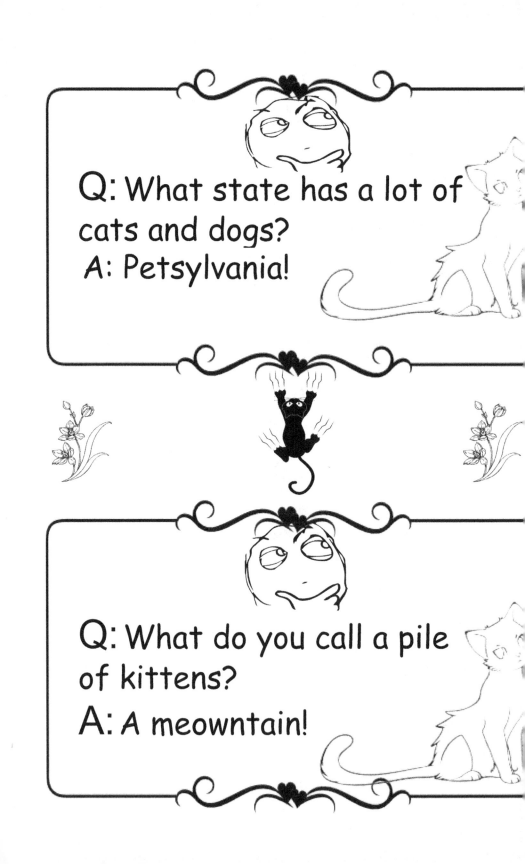

Q: What state has a lot of cats and dogs?
A: Petsylvania!

Q: What do you call a pile of kittens?
A: A meowntain!

Q: What state has a lot of cats and dogs?
A: Do-re-mew!

Q: What state has a lot of cats and dogs?
A: Do-re-mew!

Q: What's a cat's favorite subject in school?
A: Hisss-tory!

Q: What sports do cats play?
A: Hairball!

Q: What types of cats purr the best?
 A: Purrr-sians!

Q: What is it called when a cat wins a dog show?
A: A CAT-HAS-TROPHY!

Q: How do you know when your cat's done cleaning herself?

A: She's smoking a cigarette.

Q: What is it called when a cat wins a dog show?
A: A CAT-HAS-TROPHY!

Q: What do you get if you cross a leopard with a watchdog?

A: A terrified postman!

Q: What is a cat's favorite dance move?

A: The Purr-colator

Q: Did you hear about the cat who wanted to learn how to bark?

A: Curiousity killed the cat.

Q: Why was the cat so small?

A: Because it only ate condensed milk!

Q: What do you call a cat that smells good?
A: prrrr-fume.

Q: How do the Vietnamese like their soup?
A: Purrrrrfect.

Q: WWhy did the cat go to the river?
A: Claws it wanted to.

Q: What was the special offer at the pet store this week?
A: Buy 1 Cat get 1 Flea!

Q: What did the cat in the box say?
A: Get Meowt of here

Q: Wanna hear a bad cat joke?
A: Just kitten!

Q: Did you hear about the cat who swallowed a ball of yarn?

A: She gave birth to an entire litter of mittens.

Q: What's it called when a cat paints itself?
A: A self paw-trait.

Q: What's a cat's most important trait?

A: What's a cat's most important trait?!

Q: How do you make a
fashionable cat happy?

A: Give her a new purr coat
and she'll be feline good.!

Q: How does Cat-anova woo girls?

A: He just whiskers away.

Q: What do you call a cat that likes to read?

A: Litter-ate.

Q: What's the well-read cat's favorite book?

A: The Great Catsby or Of Mice And Men.

Q: What kind of sports car does a cat drive?
A: A Furrari.

Q: What do you call a cat that's a beauty influencer

A: AGlamourpuss

Q: What do you call a cat that gets anything it wants?

A: Purrr-suasive AF.

Q: What do you get if you cross a cat with Father Christmas?

A: Santa Claws!

Q: What do you call a cat that gets caught by law enforcement?

A: The purrpatrator.

Q: hat's every cat's favorite color?

A: Purrrrrrple!

Q: Why did the cat join the Red Cross?
A: She wanted to be a first-aid kit!

Q: There were 10 cats in a boat and one jumped out. How many were left?

A: None, because they were all a bunch of copycats.

Q: What did the cat say
when he went bankrupt?

A: I feel so paw!

Q: What's a cat's favorite dessert?

A: Chocolate mouse!

Q: Where does a cat go when it loses its tail?

A: The re-tail store!

Q: What do you call a cat who lives in an igloo?

A: An eskimew!

Q: How do cats stop crimes?

A: They call claw enforcement!

Q: Why was the cat so agitated?

A: Because he was in a bad mewd!

Q: What do you call a cat who loves to bowl?

A: An alley cat!

Q: What do cats love to do in the morning?

A: Read the mewspaper!

Q: How is cat food sold?

A: Usually, purr the can!

Q: What do baby cats always wear?

A: IDiapurrs!

Q: What do cats use to make coffee?

A: A purr-colator!

Q: How does a cat decide what it wants from the store?

A: It flips through the cat-alog!

Q: In what kind of weather is a vet the busiest

A: When it's raining cats and dogs!

Q: What do you call a cat wearing shoes?

A: A puss in boots!

Q: What type of cat works for the Red Cross?
A: A first aid cat!

Q: Why do cats always win video games?

A: I feel so paw!

Q: What do you call a cat wearing shoes?

A: A puss in boots!

Made in the USA
Coppell, TX
29 September 2021